The Pig and Miss Prudence

LAUREN CASTILLO 2008

By Linda Stanek

Illustrations by Lauren Castillo

STAR BRIGHT BOOKS
NEW YORK

To Alex and Elliott, with love – L.S.

For Aunt Nor – L.C.

Published in the United States of America by Star Bright Books, Inc., New York.
The name Star Bright Books and the Star Bright Books logo are registered
trademarks of Star Bright Books, Inc. Please visit www.starbrightbooks.com.

ISBN-13: 978-1-59572-125-9

Printed in China (WKT) 0 9 8 7 6 5 4 3 2 1

Library of Congress Cataloging-in-Publication Data

Stanek, Linda.
  The pig and Miss Prudence / by Linda Stanek ; illustrated by Lauren Castillo.
    p. cm.
  Summary: When Miss Prudence tries to chase a pig away from her pansies, the
result is a chaotic chase through town, upending flowers, clothes, dogs, and more.
  ISBN 978-1-59572-125-9
  [1. Pigs--Fiction. 2. Humorous stories.] I. Castillo, Lauren, ill. II. Title.

PZ7.S786355Pi 2007
[E]--dc22
                        2007033693

Miss Prudence Grimsby adjusted the cameo at the base of her collar and gazed out the window. Horses clip-clopped along the street, pulling squeaking carriages. Sunshine sparkled off gas lamps that lined the street like guards. The smell of flowers brought a smile to her face.

Her smile turned to a frown when a huge, spotted pig snuffled along the sidewalk.

"I declare," Miss Prudence said, "something should be done about these roaming pigs. They root in the garbage, they jump in front of carriages, and they upturn people's gardens. Why, they have the run of the city!"

The pig stopped to nibble Miss Prudence's pretty flowers.

Miss Prudence clenched her fists. "Not my flowers, pig!" Brandishing her parasol, she rushed outside and shouted, "Away! Away! Go away you nasty swine!"

The pig darted in front of a passing carriage. The horse reared. The driver clanged his bell. With a squeal, the frightened pig charged toward Miss Prudence.

WHAM!

Her petticoats flew in her face. She tumbled through the air and landed on the pig's back. Miss Prudence grabbed the pig's ears and held on for dear life.

The carriage driver jumped to the street. "Good heavens!" he cried. "That pig is running off with Miss Prudence! Stop pig! Bring back Miss Prudence!" The driver chased after them. . .

. . .but the pig ran on.

Miss Prudence bumpity-bumped
on the pig's back, down the road, toward a flower cart.
"Mercy me!" Miss Prudence cried.

CRASH!

Flowers and water rained from the sky. Buckets
clattered on the street. One dripping bucket plopped onto
Miss Prudence's head.

"Stop!" shouted the flower girl. "Bring back my bucket!"
She chased after them. . .

. . .but the pig ran on.

They neared the shipyard. Tall wooden masts stretched high in
the air. The pig crashed into two stevedores carrying a large crate.
"Land's sakes!" Miss Prudence cried.
The crate flew into the air. The wood splintered. Lacy underwear
scattered in the wind.

SWOOSH!

Silk drawers wrapped around Miss Prudence's
neck beneath the dripping bucket.
"Bring back those drawers!" the stevedores yelled.
They chased after them. . .

. . .but the pig ran on.

A long line of immigrants stood in a line that snaked up a hill to Castle Garden. Their tired faces lit up with surprise when Miss Prudence rode by.

The pig zipped through some open doors. It thundered through a room and headed toward a family filling out papers.

"Land O'Goshen!" Miss Prudence cried.

THUNK!

Papers flew in the air. A clothing bag soared and landed on Miss Prudence's lap, below the drawers, beneath the dripping bucket.

"Bring back our clothes, Lassie!" the father called. He chased after them. . .

. . .but the pig ran on.

Now the pig headed down the street.
Two girls were playing with rag dolls on the sidewalk.
"Good heavens!" Miss Prudence cried.
The girls stared at the galloping pig and screamed.
One girl dropped her doll.

PLOP! The doll landed on Miss Prudence's lap, atop the bag, below the drawers, beneath the dripping bucket. The girl cried, "My doll!" and burst into tears. She chased after the pig and Miss Prudence. . .

. . .but the pig ran on.

The pig fled toward the cotton mill where the
glass windows sparkled in the sun.

"Saints alive!" Miss Prudence cried, but a
door swung open and the pig careened in.

They sped past the room and through the cotton
as it spilled from the gin.

PSHT!

Cotton flew from beneath the pig's feet and landed in
Miss Prudence's lap, around the doll, atop the bag, below
the drawers, beneath the dripping bucket.

"Someone stop that pig!" a gin-worker shouted.
He chased the pig through the back door and down the street. . .

...but the pig ran on.

On the corner of Broadway, the door to Barnum's American Museum stood open and the pig veered in. General Tom Thumb leaped from a table as the pig dashed underneath.

"Deary me!" Miss Prudence cried.

YIP!

The dog who worked at the sewing machine landed with a whimper on Miss Prudence's lap, amongst the cotton, beside the doll, atop the bag, below the drawers, beneath the dripping bucket.

"Bring back my dog!" Mr. Barnum cried.
He chased the pig out the door. . .

. . .but the pig ran on.

Just three doors down, a gentleman was leaving the hat shop.
He leaped out of the way as the pig swerved into the store.

The pig whizzed between hats and umbrellas. It shot through a curtain
to the back room where milliners sewed hats balanced on wooden heads.

"Devil's mischief!" Miss Prudence cried.

A hat landed on top of the dog, who
whimpered in the cotton, beside the doll,
atop the bag, below the drawers, beneath
the dripping bucket.

WHOP!

"Stop with that hat!" the milliner cried.
She joined the crowd that chased the
pig and Miss Prudence. . .

. . .but the pig ran on.

At the Home of the Friendless, a group of orphans
gathered near the street to see the fine lady riding a pig.

A grim-faced policeman saw the pig coming and stepped
into the road. "Stop pig!" the officer ordered, but the pig
whirled 'round and plowed toward the wide-eyed youngsters.

"Have mercy!" Miss Prudence cried.

EEEE!

A girl landed on Miss Prudence's lap. She gripped the
neck of the dog, who wore the hat and whimpered in the
cotton, beside the doll, atop the bag, below the drawers,
beneath the dripping bucket.

"Release that child!" the policeman declared.
He chased after them. . .

. . .but the pig ran on.

The pig sped up the street where the steeple of Trinity Church rose into the sky. With one loud squeal, the pig bolted up the steps and into the church.

"Heaven help me!" Miss Prudence cried.

People gaped from the pews. The organ grew silent. The priest rushed down the aisle, waving his arms.

"No pigs in church!" he shouted, but the pig bowled him over.

THWACK! The priest's stole caught on the child, who gripped the dog, who wore the hat and whimpered in the cotton, beside the doll, atop the bag, below the drawers, beneath the dripping bucket. "Come back with that!" the priest shouted. He followed the pig down the steps and through the streets. . .

. . .but the pig ran on.

On and on the pig raced, the ever-growing crowd close behind.
In time, the white front of City Hall grew near.

Then up the steps the pig sprinted, down the hall and
around the corner, where it burst into the Mayor's office.

"Pity's sake!" Miss Prudence cried.
The Mayor sprang from his seat and
pounced upon the pig.

O O⁰ F!

   The bucket flew from Miss Prudence's head. The silk drawers fluttered to
the floor. The clothing bag bounced onto the desk, spilling its linens and
trews. The doll skidded across the floor. Cotton flew, like snow,
in the air. The dog slid under the Mayor's desk. The hat popped
off the dog and landed on the pig. The child sprawled belly-up.
And the priest's stole landed across the pig.

The frightened pig squealed, leaped,
and landed on the Mayor's chair. . .

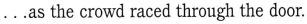

. . .as the crowd raced through the door.

Miss Prudence rose to her feet, adjusted the cameo at her throat, and placed her hands on her hips.

"I declare!" she said. "If I didn't know better, I'd say that pigs run this city!"

The pig gave a mighty squeal and scrambled to the floor. It pushed through the crowd and tore into the hall. It flew around the corner and down the steps to the bright outdoors. It kicked up its heels in the sunshine. . .

. . .and the pig ran on.